MILLIE SHARES

For Dawn

EGMONT
We bring stories to life

First published in Great Britain 2014 by Egmont UK Limited
This edition published 2018 by Dean,
an imprint of Egmont UK Limited,
The Yellow Building, 1 Nicholas Road, London, W11 4AN
www.egmont.co.uk

Text and illustration copyright © Claire Alexander 2014
Claire Alexander has asserted her moral rights.

ISBN 978 0 6035 7562 4

70161/001

Printed in Malaysia

A CIP catalogue record for this title is available from the British Library.

MILLIE SHARES

Claire Alexander

EGMONT

Millie loved her monkey.
He was her very special toy
and she would not share
him with anybody,

not even with
her best friend Lily.

"Monkey!" said Lily.

"Mine!" said Millie.

But one day at nursery, Millie forgot about Monkey.
There were so many new toys to play with.

And when she remembered him later . . .

He was gone!

Monkey wasn't very far
away. He was in the
playhouse with Lily.

"Mine!" said Lily.

Millie didn't like that one bit.

"No, mine!" she shouted.

Then Ellie, Bert and George picked up
the toys Millie had been playing with.

Millie didn't like that one bit!

"Mine!" she shouted,
snatching away the toys.

Now Millie had all the toys and her monkey,

and she played with them all by herself in the playhouse.

Suddenly she heard laughter!

"What's going on?"
she wondered.

Lily was building a huge tower
with Ellie, and Bert and George
were playing with the train set.

"I want to play!" Millie cried.

But the others thought she
would take the toys
away again . . .

No one wanted to
play with Millie.

A big tear rolled down her cheek.

Then she heard a little voice say:

"Share
Monkey?"

Millie didn't like that one bit!

But then she thought . . .

if she shared Monkey,

maybe Lily would play with her.

Share Monkey? she wondered.

Share Monkey?

"Share Monkey!" she cried.

So Millie shared
Monkey with Lily,

and they played
with him together.

Then Millie picked up
the other toys . . .

and shared them with Bert, Lily, George and Ellie.

Everyone liked playing
with Millie when she shared.

And Millie enjoyed playing
with her friends very much!

Especially her
best friend Lily!